The Little Girls' First Day at School

Illustrated by J.-L. Macias S.
Retold by J. Carruth

After the summer vacation Karen and Katy set out for school. On the way, they meet Mandy. Mandy is taking her little sister to school for the first time. Patty doesn't want to go to school. "I want to go home," she sobs. "I want my Mommy." "You must go to school," says her big sister "everyone does."

"What is the matter with Patty?" Karen asks. "She is afraid. She doesn't want to go to school," says Mandy. "I-I have a sore throat," says little Patty. "I want my Mommy."

Katy and Karen do their best to make Patty smile. But she is still sad when they go up the school steps.

"She will feel better when she sees how nice the teacher is," Karen whispers. "Wait and see." "I don't think she will," says Katy.

Katy is right. Little Patty won't even look at the blackboard. "We are going to learn about the flowers we see every day," says the teacher. "Who can draw a picture of a flower?" "I can," says Katy, leaving her desk and going up to the blackboard. "I can draw beautiful flowers."

After the lesson the children go out to play. They join hands and dance round and round.

"Come and play with us," Mandy calls. "We are having fun!" But Patty shakes her head and clutches her doll. "I don't want to play with anybody," she says.

"Leave her alone," one of the other girls laughs. "She is just a cry-baby."

School really is fun, especially at playtime. Now, little Patty would like to join in but none of the others wants to play with her.

"If you want to play with us," Mandy tells Patty, "you mustn't be a cry-baby, and you must pay attention in class." Patty sits down at her desk and works very hard. The teacher is pleased.

When school is over for the day, the teacher watches her children set out for home. "I am sure you will do well tomorrow, Patty," she calls.

"I am not a cry-baby," Patty tells her big sister that night. "I am going to be the best at school." And she reads the story for the next day's lesson.
"I think Karen and Katy and all the others will want to play with me tomorrow," she smiles.

Published in the United States and simultaneously in Canada by Joshua Morris,
431 Post Road East, Westport, CT 06
Printed in Belg